PUFFIN BOOKS

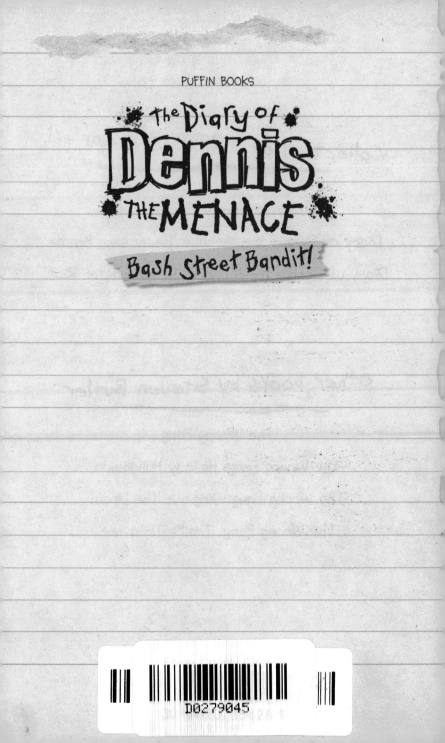

The Diary of
Dennis
THE MENACE

Bash Street Bandit!

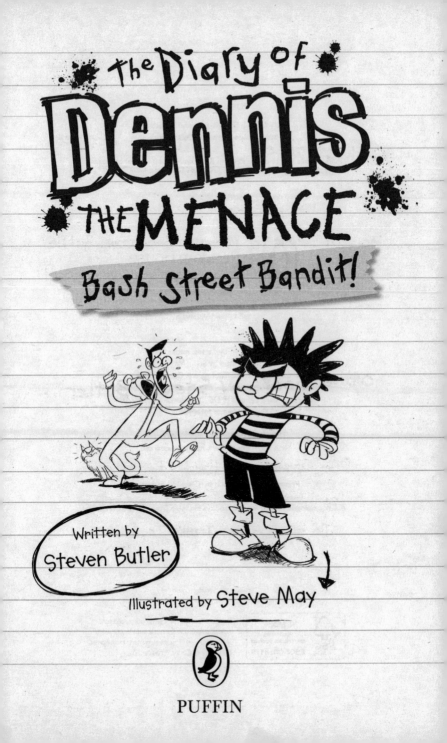

The Diary of Dennis the MENACE

Bash Street Bandit!

Written by
Steven Butler

Illustrated by Steve May

PUFFIN

PUFFIN BOOKS

UK | USA | Canada | Ireland | Australia
India | New Zealand | South Africa

Puffin Books is part of the Penguin Random House group of companies
whose addresses can be found at global.penguinrandomhouse.com.

puffinbooks.com

Penguin
Random House
UK

First published 2015
001

Written by Steven Butler
Illustrated by Steve May
Copyright © DC Thomson & Co. Ltd, 2015
The Beano ® ©, Dennis the Menace ® © and associated
characters are TM and © DC Thomson & Co. Ltd 2015
All rights reserved

Set in Soupbone
Printed in Great Britain by Clays Ltd, St Ives plc

A CIP catalogue record for this book is available from the British Library

ISBN: 978-0-141-35582-5

www.greenpenguin.co.uk

For Tom, Finn and Oliver Giles

– my merry band of Menaces

QUICK!

As soon as you look at this page, **run and hide!**
(But remember to take this book with you!)
You're about to read something seriously
shocking, my Menacing Mates. Something so
MEGA it will blow your bonce off! I hope
you've got a spare pair of pants handy cos
you're going to need them!

QUICKER!!

MOve IT!!

Hide anywhere . . .
JUST GO!!

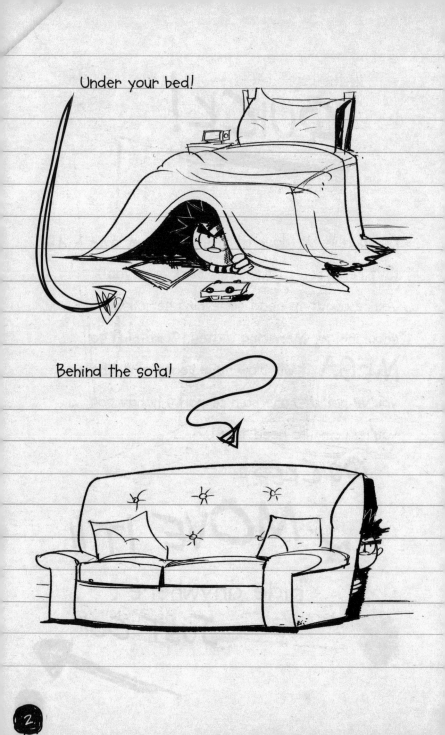

Something weirder than the weirdest

weird thing you could ever imagine

EVER is going on in Beanotown!

I don't know how to say this . . . and

you **MUSTN'T TELL ANYONE**

ELSE!

But . . .

I know what you must be thinking. That the world has gone completely **BONKERS!** How can anyone out-menace THE PRANKMASTER GENERAL?

THAT'S IMPOSSIBLE!

I thought that too, but it's true! Just a few nights ago, loads of strange things started happening around Beanotown.

Have a look at this . . . I've been cutting bits out of the *Beanotown Bugle* over the last couple of days. It's a menacing mystery!

BASH STREET BANDIT STRIKES AGAIN!

Reports are coming in of yet another SHOCKING incident!

At 7.30 a.m. Parky Bowles, the keeper of Beanotown Park, was on his morning rounds to water the flowers when he discovered something terrible. During the night, someone had dug up all the beautiful flower beds and replanted the flowers to spell out BUM-FACE!

WHO IS BEHIND THESE DREADFUL CRIMES?

Sergeant Slipper of the Beanotown Police insists that, although the criminal is still at large, they WILL be caught soon.

Replanting all the flower beds to spell
BUM-FACE!?!? It's genius! It's
MENACE-TASTIC! It's just the sort of
thing that me and my best dog-pal, Gnasher,
would do! The only problem is . . .

WE DIDN'T!

Someone out there is coming up with
TERRIFIC menacing ideas and doing them
before I've even had a chance to think them up.
How can it be happening?

I just can't imagine who's doing this . . .

There's more . . .

LOOK!

SHOCKING NEWS!

The Bash Street Bandit is causing havoc around the neighbourhood again. Late last night, as the residents of Beanotown slept peacefully in their beds, the Bandit climbed over the Colonel's fence and meddled with his impressive garden gnome collection.

Each gnome was turned upside down and had its head buried in the lawn. The Colonel woke to find a sea of little gnome bottoms sticking up in the air. A TERRIBLE SIGHT!

<u>It was brilliant!</u> I had the best view from my tree house the next morning. All those bums! The Colonel looked so confused.

But the only person more confused than the Colonel was me. The old grump lives just next door. **NEXT DOOR!** A new Menace was causing mischief right under my nose . . . AND DIDN'T ASK ME AND GNASHER TO JOIN IN!?!?

I've got to find out who's doing these amazing pranks . . . Whoever it is, they're obviously **SUPER** cool and we'll be great mates for sure . . .

The Bash Street Bandit is bound to want to join my band of merry Menaces and we'll cause happy chaos together . . .

There's always room for one more in the Menace Squad!

Maybe the Bandit is shy . . . umm . . . or if they're new in town they might not know that the **KING OF MENACES** lives nearby!

Yep . . . that's it . . . I think!

Oh . . . but what am I doing? I'm getting way ahead of myself. If this is the first time you've clapped eyes on one of my MENACING MANUALS, I should fill you in on everything that's been going on.

Are you sitting comfortably? HA!

A whole year ago, my crabby old crone of a
teacher, Mrs Creecher, made me write a diary
as a punishment for not doing my homework.
CAN YOU IMAGINE THE CRUELTY!?!?

DENNIS!

EVIL

Well, my Trainee Menaces, don't throw yourselves
down the loo in despair just yet because it
turned out to be **TERRIFIC!** I had the BEST
year and I got to document every minute of it!
Diaries are actually pretty handy . . .
There were snowstorms and fireworks and
flower-flattening battles with my archest enemy,

WALTER. There were Slopper-Gnosher-Gut-Bustin' Burgers, mega-farts, haunted houses, rollercoasters, amazing disguises AND monsters on Mount Beano!!

13.

When I finally handed in my year-long diary for Mrs Creecher to read, she went off like a rocket with a serious case of wrinkles! It was brilliant! She was so shocked by all the menacing things I'd been up to that her face turned purple and she nearly exploded. **HA!**

But that's all done with now . . . It's the school holidays and I can relax and do what all Menaces enjoy the most . . .

MENACING OF COURSE!

It's going to be great. I've got a few days to investigate and track down the Bash Street Bandit, have fun with my pals, Curly and Pie Face . . .

Something MEGA is happening! Mum and Dad are taking me and my little sister Bea on holiday . . . HOLIDAY!! It's been ages since we've had one. The only thing is, Mum and Dad won't tell us where we're going. Mum says it's going to be the best surprise **EVER!**

AGH! I can't wait . . .

But that's not for another few days, which gives me and Gnasher plenty of time to find the Bash Street Bandit. If they *are* new to Beanotown, I should give them the chance to find out all about me, **THE PRANKMASTER GENERAL.**

Tonight, after Mum and Dad have finished watching *The Great Beanotown Bake Off* on telly and have gone to bed, I'm going to sneak out and stick posters in the coolest, most menacy places around town. The Bandit is sure to see them.

IT CAN'T FAIL! Here's what I'm leaving in all the cool spots . . .

Dear Bash Street Bandit,

You lucky thing! I bet you didn't know that you're menacing in the stomping ground of the GREATEST MENACE THAT EVER LIVED!

Come and join Dennis's Menace Squad.

Meet tomorrow, 12 noon at the TOP-SECRET tree house in Dennis's back garden.

NO BUM-FACES ALLOWED.

From **Dennis**

Oh . . . bring snacks!

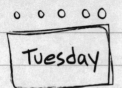

Tuesday

11.55 a.m.: I can't wait to see who the Bandit is . . . Me, Gnasher, Curly and Pie Face are all here in the tree house waiting for the new prankster to arrive. **ONLY FIVE MINUTES TO GO!** Curly even grabbed us a massive bottle of Triple-Dribble-Bubble-Pop from his mum's fridge. It's the best drink in the WHOLE WORLD and the perfect welcome treat. The Bandit is in for a SUPER BRILLIANT afternoon. **HA!**

12.25 p.m.: Ok, so the Bandit's a bit late, but will be here soon . . . any minute now . . . any minute . . .

12.30 p.m.: Hmmm . . . still no Bandit.

12.42 p.m.: Errmmm . . . well . . . maybe they're just running behind . . . y'know . . . Maybe they had an important menace to do before coming like . . . umm . . . like farting through a Softy's letterbox! That's mega important! Or . . . um . . . GAH! Where is the Bandit?

1 p.m.: Nope . . .

2 p.m.: STILL NO BANDIT . . . and Gnasher has drunk all the Triple-Dribble-Bubble-Pop. It serves the Bandit right for being so late.

3 p.m.: OH BUM!

BUM!

BUM!
BUM!
BUM!

D'you know . . . I don't think the Bash Street
Bandit is coming. There's no way they could
have missed the posters. I stuck them up
everywhere. They were in all the best, most
menacy spots around Beanotown.

Maybe the Bandit just doesn't want to join
my squad.

I . . .

I . . .

AGH! GET A GRIP, DENNIS! WHAT AM I WORRYING ABOUT?

No one, not even a grown-up, would be stupid enough **NOT** to join my MENACE SQUAD. Maybe the Bandit is just too nervous to come forward.

I AM MEGA-IMPRESSIVE AFTER ALL!

I'll just have to find the Bash Street Bandit myself. It won't take me long to figure out who it is.

I AM THE . . .

22

INTERNATIONAL MENACE
OF MYSTERY!

With my secret-agent skills, I'll find the Bandit before too long. Especially now that it's the school holidays . . . I have loads of extra time to investigate without boring old Bash Street School getting in the way of my detective work . . .

OPERATION UNMASK THE MYSTERY MENACE!

Hmmmm . . . Think, Dennis! So there's a Menace in
town who's ~~just~~ as nearly as menacy as me . . .

SO WHO IS NEARLY AS MENACY AS ME?

Not even my
pals Curly
and Pie Face
come close!

CURLY

PIE FACE

Before all this started happening, I'd have
thought nobody was as MENACING as me . . .
IT'S CRAZY!

Finding the Bandit is going to be tricky. It could be anyone . . . well . . . almost anyone.

One thing's for sure: it's easy to eliminate the people who absolutely CAN'T be the Bash Street Bandit.

Let's see . . .

First of all there's my WET-PANTED arch-enemy, Walter. Look at him . . . The bum-face of all BUM-FACES! He's as smarmy and devious as they come, but he can't be the Bash Street Bandit . . . There's just no way!

NO-NOOO-NOPE!

MASSIVE
FRAIDY CAT

Disgustingly well
behaved

HATES
Menaces

LOVES
flowers

TOTAL
BUM-FACE!

It can't be Sergeant Slipper. He's head of the Beanotown Police Department and is always trying to solve crimes, not commit them!

WAY TOO WELL BEHAVED!

Not cunning enough. Loves stopping Menaces!

There's **NO WAY** it's Mrs Creecher or Headmaster!!!! BOOKY-BORING BUM-FACES!

Too dull. Hates anything fun. Too stupid to think up menacing plans.

And it can't be the Colonel . . . Why would the old husk meddle with his own precious gnome collection? He loves those things more than anything in the world.

Poppycock! It's not me!

Well, that's the 'NO' list sorted . . . The only problem is, there are LOADS of other less boring people that COULD be the Bash Street Bandit.

I'm going to have to keep a lookout for evidence, my Trainee Menaces. If the Bandit is nearly as menacing as me, it's going to be tricky . . . **BUT!!** Even the greatest of menacing masterminds leaves the occasional clue. If I keep my eyes peeled, I'm bound to spot something.

Hmmm . . . I think it's probably a good idea to have a spot of brain food before bed. Just to make sure my powers of clue-spotting are in tip-top condition, should anything happen during the night.

I'll just make myself a teensy Double Fatties' double-fat-butter-banana-chocco-scotch sundae to take to bed with me . . .

WHAT!?!

I'm going to share it with Gnasher and . . . y'know . . . it's just for medicinal, thinky purposes.

I can already feel myself becoming a better detective!

Me and Gnasher are going to start our investigations tomorrow.

I CAN'T WAIT . . .

Wednesday

9 a.m.: Hold on to your stripes, my Menacing Mates. We're off **ALREADY!** The Bandit doesn't waste any time . . . the twisty troublemaker has been at it again.

When I came down for breakfast, Dad was fussing and grumbling over the newspaper as usual. Looks like the Bandit can't keep away from menacing. The prankster really is like me!!

UGH!

I JUST HAVE TO KNOW WHO IT IS . . .

THE BANDIT IS BACK!

The curators of the Beanotown Museum were baffled this morning when they discovered that the Bash Street Bandit had broken into the building late at night and caused Cretaceous chaos with the exhibits.

Who is behind these terrible acts of mischief? Sergeant Slipper and the Beanotown Police are baffled.

9.30 a.m.: Right! Here's the plan . . .

Later, me and Gnasher are going to check the

BUM—FACE flower beds in Beanotown Park.

There's bound to be something old Sergeant

Slipper and his policemen haven't noticed.
They're not the brainiest bunch.

But first we'd better head off to the museum
and search for clues before everything gets put
back in order.

Ha! I never thought I'd go to the Beanotown
Museum without being dragged there, kicking
and screaming, on some awful school trip.
But with my Menace's brain and my **MEGA-MENACING** detective kit we're bound to
spot something.

Oh, I just thought! You probably don't have a
MEGA-MENACING detective kit yet. Well,
don't panic! It's easy to get your hands on all
the things you'll need.

THE
PERFECT
MEGA-MENACING
DETECTIVE KIT

- **A magnifying glass**  for super-snoopy spying.

- **My Insta-Pic-Camera** that Gran bought me a few Christmases ago. It's great for snapping speedy pictures of suspicious clues. (And taking photos of your bum and sending them to your enemies!)

- **Mum's Flaky-Feet talcum powder** for fingerprint dusting.

- **A snack** for if you get hungry **(VERY IMPORTANT).**

- **A hat with funny ear flaps.** All good detectives **MUST** have a proper ear-flappy hat. I pinched mine from Dad. He likes to wear it when he goes fishing with his workmates . . .

YAWN!

11.27 a.m.: <u>HA!</u> I've just arrived at the museum and it's the best, most menace-tastic thing I've ever clapped eyes on. You should see it, my Menacing Mates. The museum was closed because of the incident and covered in Beanotown police tape . . .

The museum guides were so flustered and confused, they barely paid any attention to me and Gnasher. I just shouted, 'I'M A DETECTIVE! OUT OF MY WAY!' and walked right in. <u>HA!</u>

Now I'm inside, I can't believe my eyes!

It's a menacing marvel!

No, scratch that . . .

IT'S A MENACING MASTERPIECE!

The Bash Street Bandit is clearly a genius. **A PROPER, PROPER ONE!** Already I can really, REALLY tell that we're going to make a great team . . . when I finally figure out who it is.

The museum's ANCIENT BITS AND BOBS room has been completely menaced from top to bottom!

Better get detecting . . .

11.45 a.m.: GOT SOMETHING!! Searching for clues was a seriously tricky business, my Trainee Menaces. The Bash Street Bandit had left such a mess that it was hard to tell what was what.

We searched all over the **ANCIENT BITS AND BOBS** room and couldn't find a thing. I was about to give up when . . . GNASHER SNIFFED OUT OUR FIRST CLUE!

He started barking and growling at the T-rex's skull on the floor. At first I thought Gnasher was just making a fuss because he loves to chew bones and this one was a whopper, but then I noticed something caught in the monster's massive teeth. It was a piece of the special school notepaper used for letters to our mums

and dads . . . The kind with the Bash Street
School emblem on it. It must have got stuck
there when the Bandit was pulling off the
Tyrannosaurus's head.

Ha!
I'M ON TO YOU, BANDIT!
FOILED BY A
DENNISAURUS!!

I should have known the T-rex would come in
handy with our investigation, though. Dinosaurs
are FANTASTIC . . . even when they're
dead!! You can bet that all dinosaurs were
MEGA—MENACING back in the old—olden—
OLDY days.

I wish I had a pet dinosaur. I could train it to eat Softies and then poo on teachers. It's such a shame they're not around any more. I bet Menaces and dinosaurs were great pals back in the Dino-days . . .

What am I saying? It looks like we still are! HA!

12 noon:

CHECK . . .

CHECK . . .

OVER . . .

This is Detective Dennis and his trusty hound, solving crimes and getting one step closer to finding the Bash Street Bandit.

Our first clue is a scrap of school notepaper. So one thing's for sure . . . the Bandit must go to Bash Street School.

Hmmm . . .

KEEP MENACING!

49

We may be one step closer, Menacing Mates, but we're not close enough. Loads of people go to Bash Street School. On the last day of term, Mrs Creecher gave us a ton of **BORING** letters about this, that and such-'n'-such to take home for our mums and dads to read.

Anyone with half a brain would have squished them up into little balls with their spit and fired them at the back of Creecher's head with their pea-shooter, but there's probably loads still lying around in the bottom of people's school bags.

The Bandit must have had a school letter stuffed in a pocket or backpack or something. That means it could be anyone. **UGH!** EVEN WALTER!?!? **Ha!** What am I saying? Of course it's not Walter.

ONWARDS, MY MENACE SQUAD!

We'll have to look for more clues down at
Beanotown Park. I'd better get over there and
have a poke around.

We'll figure out who the Bandit is before you
can say BUM—FACE!!!

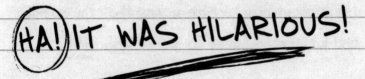

3 p.m.: What did I tell you, my Trainee
Menaces? When I got to Beanotown Park, there
was a big crowd of people, all chatting and
gawping at the **BUM—FACE** flower beds.

(HA!) IT WAS HILARIOUS!

It looked like half the town was there to get a look at the Bandit's handiwork. Even Walter! Yep! Lord Softy McSoftison was right at the front of the crowd, wailing and gnashing his teeth about how terrible it was that the roses and pansies had been tampered with. HA!

Normally I'd steer clear of Walter and his

booky, BUM-FACED cronies, Bertie and Dudley,

but I noticed they were talking to Parky Bowles,

the park keeper. I crept as close as I could

and hid myself behind one of the bins near the

flower beds to have a good listen.

AHA! So the Bandit broke into Parky Bowles's gardening shed to find the tools to dig up all the flowers. I think I'd better start looking in there.

This is Detective Dennis on the trail. I'll let you know what I find . . .

3.25 p.m.: *I DID IT!* I found our second clue and it's a SUPER juicy one. My detective skills are better than ever. Thank goodness for the Double Fatties' double-fat-butter-banana-chocco-scotch sundae I had last night. It's clearly the best brain food a Menace can eat!

ANYWAY, I managed to sneak into Parky's
shed when he wasn't looking and have a good
rummage around. There was just a load of
rusty old shovels and rakes and hoes and not
much else, except spiderwebs and mouse poo.
It all seemed pretty hopeless when suddenly
I spotted . . . there . . . on the wall . . .

THE BANDIT HAD LEFT A WHITE,
CHALKY HANDPRINT!

Thanks to my MEGA
Insta-Pic-Camera, I got
a good photograph of it
for evidence . . .

CLUE NUMBER 2

Chalky handprint

KEEP MENACING!

The Bash Street Bandit was using chalk right before breaking into Parky Bowles's gardening shed. It also explains the chalk writing on the wall at the museum. That's got to narrow it down, surely?

THINK, DENNIS!!

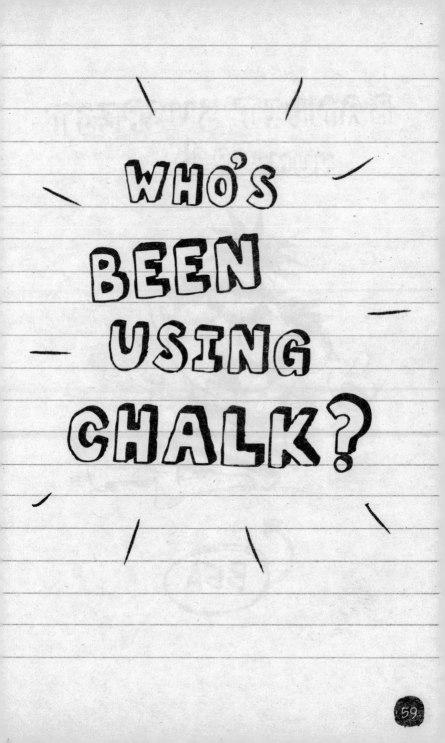

I know my little sister Bea loves to play with her chalks at home. She's always drawing all over her bedroom walls with them and making Mum go bananas.

It couldn't be my little sister, could it? She's certainly a mini-Menace AND she's learned from the best. But Bea doesn't go to Bash Street School yet and wouldn't be tall enough to climb up and reach the T-rex skull in the museum!

Just two days ago, I saw Minnie
drawing Hop-the-Bog-Frog
games on the pavement outside
Mr Har Har's Joke Shop.

Minnie is a **SUPER** menacy **MINX**.
She could definitely be the Bash
Street Bandit!

This is growing more and more
MYSTERIOUS by the minute.

The Bandit goes to Bash Street School
and was using chalk right before they
replanted the Beanotown Park flower
beds. **Hmmm . . .**

There's only one thing for it, my Menace Detective Squad. If me and Gnasher are going to rack our brains and figure out who the Bash Street Bandit really is, we're going to need EVEN more sweet, sugary brain food. HA!

I'm off home to have a think and eat myself smarter. Catch you later . . .

Midnight:

STOP
EVERYTHING!!!

I . . .

 I . . . .

 I can't believe it . . . .

It's too shocking . . . My brain might explode.

Something . . . Something . . .

OH, SPIT IT OUT, DENNIS!

Something MEGA happened earlier tonight. It's

all a bit of a blur . . . I . . . I would have blown

my bonce off with surprise if I wasn't so brave.

After all this . . . the Bandit is . . . is . . . is a

BUM-FACED ENEMY!

Let me explain . . . It was ten o'clock and I was sitting on my bed with Gnasher, eating my way through a third helping of minty-creamy-crumble-crunch ice cream when we heard the most enormous scream.

It was massive and squeaky and irritating and I knew straight away who it belonged to. The only person that can shriek that high in all of Beanotown is . . .

WALTER!

AAAAH!

By the time I darted downstairs and ran out into the front garden, half the street was awake and coming outside to see what all the hoo-ha was about.

Walter was in front of his house, wearing his teddy-bear onesie and being a right Whingey-Wet-Pants! He was wailing like you've never heard anyone wail before . . . like a demented **Softy rooster!**

I ran over to get a better look and saw that he was kneeling over something furry on the ground. As all the neighbours started gathering round, Walter picked the furry thing up and we realized that it was his pampered pussycat, Claudius.

OH 'ECK!

WHAT'S GOING ON?

At first I had no idea what was going on.
Walter just kept screaming and crying. But
then he turned Claudius round and . . .

HAAAAA!!!!

I couldn't help but laugh. **BUM-FACE** is one
of the funniest **words** in the world, second
only to **BOTTOM-BURP, KNICKERS** and
PIDDLE-PANTS!! How could I not laugh?

It really was genius . . . Changing the flower
beds in Beanotown Park to say **BUM-FACE**
was one thing, but shaving it into the fur of
WALTER'S CAT was something else.
It was **BRILLIANT!**

But . . . I bet you're wondering what I was
talking about before. How can the Bandit be a
bum-faced enemy when they'd just pulled off
the best prank Beanotown has ever seen on
the most irritating

WHINGEY-WILFRED EVER?

Well, hold on to your knickers and I'll tell you . . .

It was just then that everything went wrong!! **EVERYTHING!!** Walter, that little smarmer, turned on me quicker than Gnasher on a fresh can of Gristly-Giblet-Jumble dog food!

Like I said, I couldn't help laughing at Walter and his *purrrr*-fect cat . . . It was SO funny! The only problem was, Wet-Lettuce-Walter didn't find it quite as hilarious as I did. Before I knew it, he spun round, pointed at me and started shouting . . .

Walter just blew his bonce off! He was
sweating and pointing and wouldn't stop
shouting, 'YOU'RE ALWAYS MENACING ME,
DENNIS! YOU DID THIS! YOU DID THIS!'
Well, you can guess what happened next . . .

Every stupid grown-up in the crowd started
staring at me and looking angry. Why do
grown-ups believe everything they're told?
Anyone with half a brain would NEVER listen
to a Whinge-Bottom like Walter! But they all
did . . . Even Mum and Dad were glaring at me
and shaking their heads!

In no time at all, Sergeant Slipper showed up
and started asking questions.

It was AWFUL, my Menacing Mates . . .

I thought I was RUINED!

DONE FOR!!

I didn't even have time to run like the wind before Sergeant Slipper put me in handcuffs . . . HANDCUFFS! For a nanosecond, I saw my whole life flash before my eyes.

That part was BRILLIANT, but then I saw what the future of the human race would be like if it was deprived of my MENACY BRILLIANCE! Imagine a world without me, THE INTERNATIONAL MASTER OF MENACING, in it? There would be no one to train up future Menaces. No one to hold off the hordes of skipping, sappy, smarmy SOFTIES. It was like watching a TERRIFYING, flower-filled horror movie.

Imagine it . . . Years in the future and Lord
Softitron has taken over the world and turned
everyone into flower-loving bum-faces!

In the Menace-less future, there are bum-faces everywhere you turn. People even have bum-faced babies!

It was just too horrible!

Slipper was about to cart me off to Beanotown Police Station. I would have been thrown in jail for certain if it hadn't been for what happened next . . .

DUN-DUN-DAAAH!

Just as I was about to abandon all hope of ever menacing again, there came another bigger wail, **EVEN LOUDER** than Walter's screaming. It was **SO** loud that everyone spun round.

It was coming from my tree house, over the other side of the road, and I knew that **IT WAS GNASHER.**

Now Gnasher has loads of types of howls and I recognize and understand all of them. This one was a very particular howl indeed. Let me explain . . .

Menacing Lesson no. 9987: A good Menace always understands his dog.

Your dog can get you out of even the worst scrapes if you know what to listen for. Pay special attention to what it's saying.

DENNIS'S DOG-HOWL DICTIONARY!

First there's the **HOOOOOOOOO!** kind of howl. That means 'I want a Slopper-Gnosher-Gut-Bustin' Burger **NOW** or I'll probably die of hunger . . . or **BITE** you!' Obviously . . .

Then there's the **RRAAAOOORR!** kind of howl. That means 'BEA'S FARTED! DIVE FOR COVER!'

The **RUUUUUUUGH!** kind of howl means 'Walkies . . . PLEASE!?!?'

And the **GROOOOOOOR!** kind of howl means 'Teachers! RUN FOR IT!'

BUT . . .

There's one kind of howl that's saved for only the **WORST OF MENACING EMERGENCIES.** It's the

WoWoWoWoWoWo!

kind and that's the exact same howl that Gnasher was using.

My heart froze . . . I knew something **TERRIBLE** must have happened. Something more terrible than the most terrible, **TERRIBLE** thing that ever happened in the world. Scratch that . . .

THE UNIVERSE!

It was just then that I remembered that SOFTY SERGEANT SLIPPER was a crinkly old grown-up. He couldn't stop me . . . I'm DENNIS THE MENACE! Before he could even think about grabbing me, I wriggled out of his adult-sized handcuffs and darted between his legs.

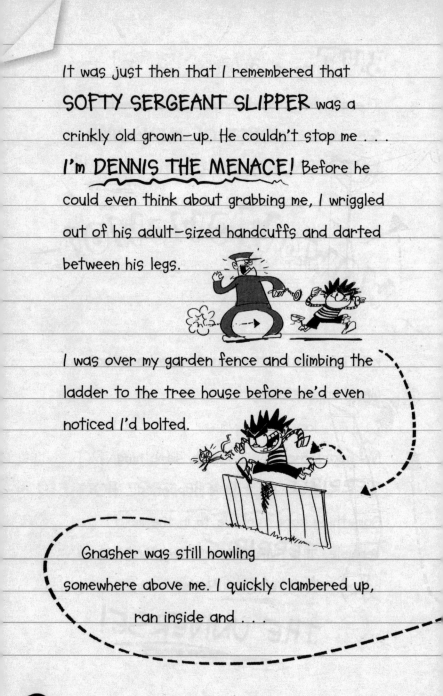

I was over my garden fence and climbing the ladder to the tree house before he'd even noticed I'd bolted.

Gnasher was still howling somewhere above me. I quickly clambered up, ran inside and . . .

— WARNING! —

What you are about to read will make your head blow off with **shock!!!**

My Menacing Mates, it was a **TERRIBLE** sight. At first I thought I must have gone stark raving batty. How could it be true?

While we were all across the road, looking at Walter wailing at his fat cat's new haircut, **THE BANDIT MENACED THE TREE HOUSE!!!**

THE MASTER OF MENACING WAS MENACED! How could this have happened? It was chaos . . .

The Bandit even unravelled my spare Menace's sweater!

Poor Gnasher had
been tied up with
a stripy Bash
Street School tie.

My squashed bug
collection had been
RE-SQUASHED!

I had to give Gnasher three extra helpings of ice cream after all that. My poor **GNASH-TASTIC** pal was pretty shaken. Unfortunately, he had his head buried in a box of Poppin' Jammy Sour-Candy Toaster Tarts when the Bandit struck so he didn't get a good look or sniff at the tree-house trasher.

I've never heard of anything like it. Who would be crazy enough to menace the best pet-pals of the King of the Softies **AND** THE PRANKMASTER GENERAL on the same night?

The plot has just got a whole lot thicker, my Trainee Menaces. Thicker than the gloppy gravy in the Bash Street School canteen. **And that's REALLY thick!**

Hmmm . . .

I'm going to have a quick think. Let's look at the evidence . . .

CLUE
NUMBER 3
A piece of
stripy tie

CLUE
NUMBER 2
Chalky
handprint

KEEP MENACING!

It just makes no sense . . . Who would be the enemy to Softies AND Menaces? The stripy tie that Gnasher was tied up with is a

SUPER
BIG
CLUE!

But everyone from Bash Street School has got one of those . . . even the teachers! So who could it be?!

BANDIT SUSPECT
NUMBER 3

ANGEL
FACE

Angel Face is Headmaster's daughter and is only
interested in her own mischief. She'd definitely
menace me and Walter on the same night. I bet
Headmaster has loads of stripy ties too . . .
It would be easy for Angel Face to pinch one.

Spotty, 'Erbert, Smiffy and Fatty from Bash Street all wear stripy ties. Hmmmm . . . but everyone knows they do. They'd be practically handing themselves in . . . The Bash Street kids would never menace a Menace, would they?

The Bash Street Bandit must be **INSANE! BONKERS!** LOOP-DE-LOOPY-LOOP!! Who would menace Softies and Menaces at the same time?

What . . . what if . . . what if the Bandit has come to steal my menacing crown?

What if they've come to overthrow me and rule Beanotown forever? I'll be humiliated. No Menace would ever take me seriously **AGAIN!**

NO SOFTY would ever take me seriously again either.

THIS IS BAD, my Menacing Mates.

Sergeant Slipper let me off the hook after he saw that I'd been menaced too, but only for now. I know that old GRUMP still thinks I'm guilty . . . and Walter does too. If I'm going to stop the Bandit before I get thrown in Beanotown Jail, I'll have to work quickly . . .

Really quickly!

THE
BANDIT BALLOON

Giant balloon filled with Bea's mega-farts.

I wait for the Bandit to sniff out the bait and cut the rope from behind the bush.

Slopper–Gnosher–Gut–Bustin' Burger . . . No true Menace can resist them.

BYE–BYE, BANDIT!

Thursday

8.30 a.m.:

AAAAAAAAAAAAGGGGGGHHHHHH!

In all the Bandit-finding excitement,
I completely forgot we're going on HOLIDAY
today. Mum just shouted up the stairs and told
me to bring my suitcase down to the front door.

SUITCASE?

I haven't even STARTED packing my menacing
holiday essentials . . . and **WHAT ABOUT
THE BANDIT?**

If I'm out of Beanotown, the Bash Street Bandit will be free to cause chaos wherever they choose. What if my tree house is wrecked again? What if they take over my **TOP-SECRET** fort in the junkyard?

I don't even have time to build the Bandit Balloon I invented.

UGH! It's horrible, but there's no use worrying about it, I suppose. The Bandit will still be here when I get back and will probably have left a load of new clues by then . . .

COME ON! CHEER UP, DENNIS, YOU'RE GOING ON HOLIDAY!

I'm going to have the best time of my life . . . I just know it!

Mum and Dad still won't tell me and
Bea where we're going, which means
it must be somewhere

SUPER,

SUPER

AWESOME!!

Time to get packed or Mum will
throw a wobbly. I'd better not leave
anything to chance.

Let's think . . . .

HOLIDAY
ESSENTIALS

- Shark-repellent spray.
- Yeti-spotting guidebook.
- Masks and snorkels for deep-sea menacing.
- Catapult with EXTRA mud-ball ammo, in case of local Softies.
- Safari camouflage sweater.
- Inflatable crocodile for pool-time fun.
- Ropes for mountain climbing.
- Inflatable dinghy for white-water rafting.
- Flameproof pants, in case of volcanoes.
- Extra-Sour-Candy Toaster Tarts for desert island survival.
- Lion-bite antiseptic cream.

8.45 a.m.: Right, that's all done . . . **Agh!**
I can't wait! It wasn't easy getting all my
holiday essentials into one case, but I managed
it with a little help from Gnasher.

9.30 a.m.:

BLAST OFF!

Dad bundled our things on to the roof of the car and we were away. I can't wait to see where they're taking us.

I've never seen my parents look so excited. They still won't tell us where we're going, but Mum's practically eating her own head with happiness. This is going to be **TERRIFIC!**

Since I have the best detective skills in the world and probably the biggest brain as well . . . probably . . . I've narrowed our holiday destination down to a few final choices. It just has to be one of them . . .

Yep, it's definitely one of those holiday destinations . . . I'd bet my stripes on it!

I'll let you know when we arrive, my Trainee Menaces . . .

IT'S SO EXCITING!!!!!

9.37 a.m.: That's weird. Dad has just driven the car over the bridge by the river. The only thing over that bridge is Mount Beano and the woods . . . Oh well . . . We must be driving straight over the top of it and onwards to our TREMENDOUS holiday destination.

9.41 a.m.:

Ummm . . . Dad is slowing the car down . . .

I . . .

I . . .

NOOOOOOOOOOOOO!!!

Is this some cruel joke? Are Mum and Dad playing a trick or have they gone round the bend? It's too awful . . . It's too terrible . . . It's **TOO BORING!**

I have two words for you, my Menacing Mates. The most dreadful words there have ever been in the history of really, really, **REALLY** boring words.

THE COUNTRYSIDE!

Mum and Dad have brought us camping at

the holiday park next to Beanotown Lake.

That's it. No tropical jungle islands . . .

No adventures at the bottom of the sea . . .

How am I going to use my SHARK-REPELLENT

SPRAY when we're camping in Beanotown Woods?

Mum says I should be grateful because the

countryside is a beautiful thing . . .

BEAUTIFUL? BRAIN-NUMBING, more

like! There aren't any cool animals around here.

Where are the KILLER SPIDERS or GIANT

ANGRY RHINOS? Nothing exciting EVER happens

in the countryside.

You'd be lucky to get **ants in your sandwiches** and **squirrel poo in your sleeping bag!** This is going to be the worst holiday of my life. I'm stuck at Beanotown Campsite in the middle of the woods while the Bash Street Bandit is probably riffling through my top-secret stuff and stealing my menacing crown.

MY LIFE IS OVER!

I'll probably be dragged off by skipping, singing chipmunks in my sleep, or I'll get Boredom-Brain-Rot and they'll find me in fifty years' time living in a cave on Mount Beano, wearing nothing but a leaf and the longest beard in history.

10 a.m.: Already bored . . . Suddenly those skipping chipmunks seem like a treat!

10.27 a.m.:

Can barely keep my eyes open . . .

So . . .

Much . . .

Green . . .

10.56 a.m.: Does anyone know how to attract ferocious Menace—eating badgers?

11 a.m.: Given up hope of having my head bitten off by Menace—eating badgers . . . Mum and Dad have been fiddling around with the tent for over an hour now. That'll serve 'em right! **Ha!** Dad looks like a furious tomato (his face is so red!) and Mum is all tangled up in the support ropes.

I suppose this is slightly making up for the disappointment of camping. HA!

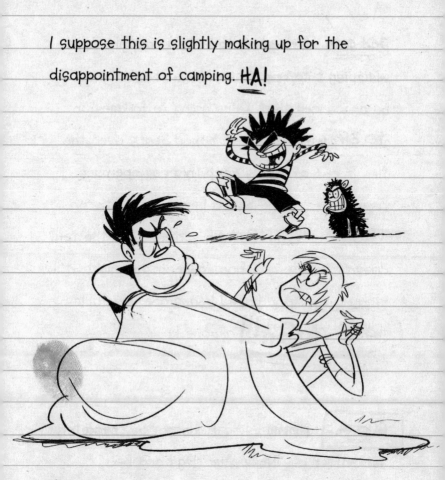

4 p.m.: After six hours of pulling, groaning, sweating, grumbling, heaving and saying rude words that mums and dads aren't supposed to say, the tent is up.

Dad says we're going to build a campfire next,
which isn't so bad, I suppose . . . but then
he announces that we're going to forage for
forest greens and cook baked beans over the
fire in one of Mum's rusty old camping pans.
Forest greens and baked beans . . . With my
TRUMP—TASTIC little sister??? If the tent
doesn't inflate and float away in the night, it'll
be a miracle! And baked beans are vegetables
too . . . **AGH!!!**

6 p.m.: Hmmm . . . I may not be completely
sunk after all. While Mum, Dad and Bea
tucked into their baked beans, me and Gnasher
sneaked off and found the campsite shop over
at the far end, by the lake.

<u>GUESS WHAT?!?!</u> They sell Greasy-Battered-Turkey-Twists like the ones from Bash Street School canteen. Turkey-Twists are one of the few edible things that Olive the dinner lady serves up at lunchtime.

I can easily survive on Greasy-Battered-Turkey-Twists while we're out in all this . . . this nature . . . and they have no vegetables in them whatsoever! **DELICIOUS!** Luckily, I brought my week's pocket money with me. That should just about cover my Turkey-Twist rations for the next few days.

This is survival at its most

EXTREME!

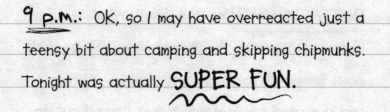

9 p.m.: OK, so I may have overreacted just a teensy bit about camping and skipping chipmunks. Tonight was actually SUPER FUN.

Mum and Dad took me and Bea to the observatory up on the top of Mount Beano. At first I thought it was going to be mega boring and a proper snoozefest, but it turned out to be brilliant!

The telescope on the front of the observatory is **HUGE** and you can see all the stars and planets like they're right in front of you.

I bet no one has ever taught you about all the different menacing constellations in the sky, have they? Of course they haven't! There isn't a teacher in the world who is cool or brainy enough to know about them. Well, listen carefully, my Trainee Menaces. I'll give you a quick crash course.

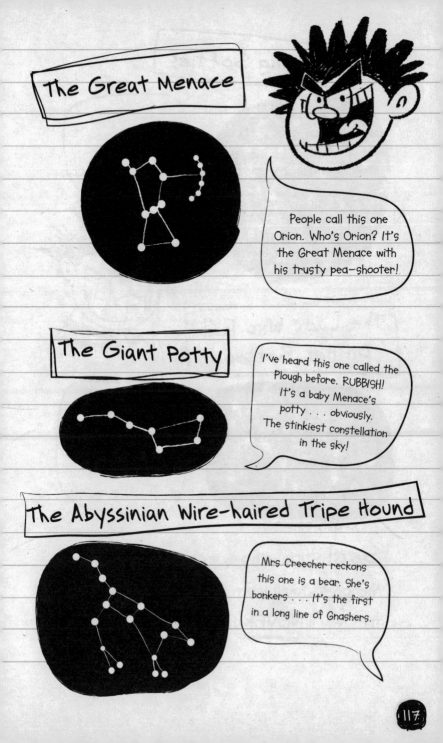

The Skipping Softies

Some people call this one the Twins. Twins? Look again!

The Lady Who Fell On Her Bottom

This one is sometimes known as Virgo. Dad says it's named after an ancient Roman snooker player, but he's wrong . . .

See! Stick with me, my merry band of Menaces. You'll learn things from my diaries that you'll **NEVER** hear in school.

10 p.m.: Mum's making us all go to bed EARLY . . . but it's not too bad. Dad's promised to take us out on a boat on the lake tomorrow so the sooner we're asleep, the sooner we can do some more fun things.

There are stories of the great Beanotown Lake monster that lives down in the deepest parts of the lake.

People have been coming here for years from all over the world to try and get a photograph of it. I bet lake monsters would LOVE Menaces.

If the monster's out there, it's bound to show itself for me . . . With my trusty Insta-Pic-Camera, I'll probably get a great shot and become a squillionaire.

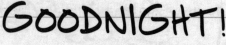

Maybe camping is pretty

MENACE-TASTIC

after all . . .

GOODNIGHT!

Friday

8 a.m.: UGH! Something . . . something's happening . . . I just woke up and the ground is shaking. At first I thought it was just Dad's snoring, but it's not. It's something

BIG!

I'm going to investigate, my Trainee Menaces.

I'll report back as soon as I've seen what's causing it . . .

8.30 a.m.:

I ... I ... can't ... believe ...

I CAN'T BELIEVE THIS ...

I must be cursed or something. Surely no one in the world is having worse luck than me at the moment?

FORGET the Bash Street Bandit!!

FORGET nature and bird-watching and flipsy, fluttery butterflies!!

I've just seen the most devastating sight
OF MY LIFE!

I crawled out of the tent to find out what was
making the ground shake and came face to face
with the most enormous camper van I've ever
laid eyes on. It was massive!

IT WAS BIGGER

THAN A BUS . . .

It drove right up and parked next to our
tent . . . and then . . . and then the door
flew open . . . and . . .

Walter's family have plonked themselves next door to our tent. It's bad enough living so near that **BUM–FACE** in Beanotown! I can't bear having him right by me on holiday as well.

IT'S RUINED!!

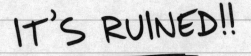

AND . . . to make it even worse . . . Walter's holiday home on wheels is unbelievable. Just after they parked, Walter's dad came out and clicked a little remote control with a red button on it and the whole thing sort of . . . UNFOLDED! It's . . . it's . . . IT'S NOT FAIR! Why is **THE PRANKMASTER GENERAL** stuck in a tiny tent with his snoring mum and dad and farting little sister when Walter's family arrive in total style? You should have seen it!

I can barely bring myself to say this, but
Walter's holiday home is the coolest thing
I have **EVER** seen.

That Smarmy—Smarmer was up on the top deck
birdwatching with a huge grin on his face . . .
Until he saw me. **HA!**

Then he got all scared and started crying for
his mumsie! He was wailing, 'It's that hooligan,
Dennis! The Bash Street Bandit has followed us
here!'
Can you believe it?!

UGH! He's such a BUM—FACE!
Walter knows I can't be the Bandit. How could
I be when we were both menaced on the same
night? He's just sticking to his story because

he knows he can get me in trouble. Sergeant Slipper believes anything that Walter and his posho mum and dad say. They're **SO** ANNOYING!

Menacing Lesson no. 9999:
Softies will do their best to ruin your fun at every opportunity. Make sure you stay one step ahead and ruin theirs first!

After Walter kept on shouting, his dad put down his barbecue tongs, grabbed a rolled-up newspaper and started shooing at me like I was some stray cat.

SHOOING ME!?!?! It'll take more
than a Softy waving a newspaper to make
THE KING OF THE MENACES run away.

Oh well, now that they're here, I might as well
have some fun. It's not like Walter doesn't
deserve it . . . Just this year alone he's tried
to scare me with a fake Halloween party at
Number 13 Frightville Avenue, filled Beanotown
with flowers to attract hordes of skipping
Softies and tried to trick me out of being the
first person in the world to ride the Vomit
Comet at Beanoland theme park. He's a devious
little whinger.

Hmmm . . . I think it's time I repay Walter
for pointing the finger at me in front of
Sergeant Slipper.

2 p.m.: So we're out on Beanotown Lake in one of the little wooden boats that Dad hired from the campsite shop.

It's brilliant! Just after the

newspaper—waving incident, I heard Walter's family talking about going out on the lake as well for a spot of fishing. I got straight to work and slipped a note under their holiday—home door . . .

I made a copy just in case.

LOOK!

Dear ~~Bum~~ Faces Holidaymakers,

Just a letter to warn you that if you go out on Beanotown Lake you run the risk of being eaten by the lake monster. Sightings are becoming more and more frequent, and it especially loves the taste of El Snobbo Caviar and bow ties.
You have been warned.

Beanotown Campsite Manager

I knew Walter would fall for it. He's such a fraidy squirrel!

Just before Mum and Dad went to hire our boat, I saw Walter and his parents marching off to get theirs. Walter was crying and moaning, 'No, Dadsie, I don't want to get eaten . . . PLEASE!'

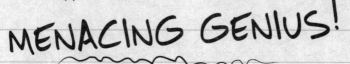

It was
HILARIOUS!

What happened next was a stroke of

MENACING GENIUS!

(Even if I do say so myself.)

Once we'd rowed round the lake a few times,
Mum and Dad got tired of pulling the oars and
decided to take a little nap. That's when me
and Bea struck. I love my little sister. She's
turning out to be a right menacing marvel.

We waited until Walter and his family were happily fishing and then we made use of the inflatable crocodile I packed for pool playtime . . . and it's a good thing I brought those masks and snorkels after all.

Ha! You should have seen Prince Smarmsalot's face when he reeled in the deflated crocodile . . . **AGH!**

That's when Bea let rip with her greatest talent . . .

HA! I've never seen anyone row to shore so fast . . . That'll teach Walter for being such a **BUM—FACE** and his dad for waving a newspaper at me. Like that's going to frighten me . . .

UGH! THE NEWSPAPER!

In all this **HOLIDAY HILARITY**, I've completely forgotten about the Bandit. I need to get back to Walter's camper van and get a look at that paper. Maybe the Bash Street Bandit has struck again . . .

I won't be long, my merry band of Menaces. I'll keep you posted . . .

8.30 p.m.: Ugh! Thank goodness Walter's family are all Softies and go to bed super early. I could see the newspaper on the table by the barbecue, but Walter's mum and dad sat next to it the whole evening. The minute they toddled off, I grabbed it. Walter didn't come outside once. Ha! I heard his mum saying that he'd locked himself in the bathroom and wouldn't show his face!!!

Anyway . . . have a

LOOK at this!

THE BASH STREET BANDIT HAS STRUCK AGAIN AND CAUSED UTTER CHAOS AT THE BEANOTOWN LIBRARY!

During the night, the Bandit broke in and switched the dust jackets of every single book in the building.

One startled victim had this to say:

'I checked *Knitting For Beginners* out of the library, but when I got it home and opened it, it was *How to BELCH in Spanish* . . . I was SO startled!'

Who is committing these terrible crimes?

It's so strange . . . Every time the Bandit has struck, it's always been in a place of interest to **BORING, BOOKY BUM-FACES.**

There was . . .

- The **flower beds** in Beanotown Park
- The Colonel's gnome collection
- **Beanotown Museum**
- Walter's house
- **My tree house** (every <u>BUM—FACED</u> Softy would love to get a look in there)
- And now Beanotown Library

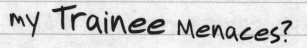

What am I missing, my Trainee Menaces?

I wish I was back in Beanotown right now. I can't

solve anything from up here on Mount Beano.

Hmmm . . . if only I could get hold of Walter's

binoculars. That way I might have a chance of

spying down into . . .

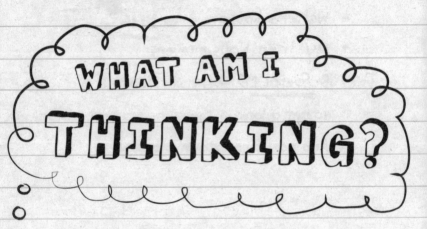

WHAT AM I THINKING?

I don't need Walter's rubbish little binoculars!

I've got the best piece of spying equipment in all

of Beanotown right under my nose . . .

THE OBSERVATORY!

Quick!

10.17 p.m.:

CHECK . . .

CHECK . . .

OVER . . .

CHECK!

This is Secret Agent Dennis

reporting live from the Mount Beano observatory.

Getting in was a piece of cake thanks to my
bestest pooch-pal. When we arrived, the doors
were all padlocked shut, but Gnasher bit through
them like they were made of jelly.

Here goes . . . I think I can figure out how
to work this telescope thing. Let's try something
easy to start with . . .

<u>Ha!</u> There's my room. BRILLIANT!

So we know the Bash Street Bandit only strikes in places that Softies are interested in . . . Um . . . how about . . . Headmaster's house?

Ugh! YUCK! Headmaster is so weird, but that's normal! All headmasters are weird. Nothing out of the ordinary there . . .

Ummm, how about the town hall? Softies love it there . . .

Nothing strange going on there . . .

I KNOW!!!

School is irresistible to Softies . . . they love it! CAN'T GET ENOUGH!

Nothing on the climbing frame . . .

Everything looks normal in the school canteen . . .

How about . . .?

GUH! THE BANDIT IS
MENACING OUR CLASSROOM!!!

HA! Mrs Creecher is going to be so angry . . .

I HAVE TO CATCH THE BANDIT! I'VE
GOT TO GET BACK TO TOWN . . .

AND PRONTO!!!

Midnight:

WOW!
W-O-W!!

What a night . . . That was one of the craziest things that has ever happened to me, my Menacing Mates. You won't believe it when I tell you . . .

After spotting the Bandit in our classroom, I raced back to the campsite to get Bea and Gnasher. If I was going to catch the Bandit once and for all, I needed my **MENACE SQUAD** with me.

First things first, we had to find some wheels. There was no way we'd make it in time if we ran . . . **We needed some serious speed.** I grabbed Bea's pushchair out of the back of Dad's car, but it was no use. Oh . . . it had wheels, but it wasn't nearly big enough for me, Bea and Gnasher to get in together.

That's when I had a **MEGA** idea. We needed something big enough to fit all of us and fast enough to get us into town before the Bandit finished menacing Bash Street School.

THE CATCH-THE-BANDIT-MOBILE

Bea's turbo-powered wind for acceleration

Pop!

Walter's family hot tub

The wheels from Bea's pushchair

Attaching the wheels to Walter's hot tub was **SUPER** easy. I got a few of Dad's tools from the car and I can be mega quiet when I work because I'm an **INTERNATIONAL MENACE OF MYSTERY.** The big problems started when I pulled the plug to drain the water out and it sloshed all over the deck and washed the barbecue over the edge with a massive

Before I could do anything, Walter ran out on to the pool deck and caught us red-handed.

Walter looked like he'd seen a ghost . . .

A GHOST TRYING TO STEAL HIS HOT TUB!

He went **BANANAS** and ran towards us,
flailing his hands around like a daddy-
long-legs . . . and then . . . then Walter
did something I wasn't expecting. He jumped
into the tub!

He was wailing and yelling, 'I'VE CAUGHT
YOU, DENNIS! YOU ARE THE BASH
STREET BANDIT!'

Well, I wasn't about to let Whingey-Wet-Pants
stop me when we were so close to nabbing the
Bandit. Walter would soon see that it wasn't
me if he came with us, so I turned to Bea and
shouted, **'NOW!'**

IT WAS AMAZING! There's no turbo
power in the world like a gassy little sister.

We went tearing downhill towards the town and Bash Street School! It was faster than the Vomit Comet rollercoaster!!

Gnasher sat at the front and sounded the alarm to alert the whole of Beanotown. If we were going to catch the Bandit, I wanted everyone there to see it.

We'd nearly reached the school gates when I suddenly realized we had no brakes. I forgot to build any on the

Catch-the-Bandit-Mobile!!! The only way to stop was to crash straight into the school gates . . . IT WAS MEGA!

When we'd finally untangled ourselves
and clambered out of Walter's runaway
hot tub, I saw loads of the other kids
from school coming out of their houses
in their pyjamas. I can always count on
Gnasher to raise the alarm.

I ran ahead to the front doors of
the school and saw that someone had
picked the lock with what looked like a
brooch pin.

What kind of kid
        wears a **brooch**?

I peeked inside and everything was dark and silent. There's something **SUPER** creepy about being in school when it's dark, so I was mega pleased when I saw Minnie, the Bash Street Kids and Angel Face arrive at the gates behind me.

I WASN'T
SCARED
OR ANYTHING . . .
I was just really pleased . . . that's all!

I quickly whispered what was going on to everyone and we all went in together. Even Walter came along!

We sneaked down the hall towards our classroom. Luckily, Angel Face had brought a torch so we could see where we were going.

When we got to our classroom
door, we could hear noises coming
from inside, so we sneaked up and
pushed it open quietly.

AND THAT,
MY MENACING MATES,
IS WHEN IT ALL
HAPPENED!!

Minnie reached inside the door and
flicked the light on and . . .

It was <u>Creech!</u> She had her back to us and was writing BUM-FACE on the chalkboard . . .

Mrs Creecher!?!?

Walter suddenly plucked up a gust of courage from somewhere and stepped into the room . . .

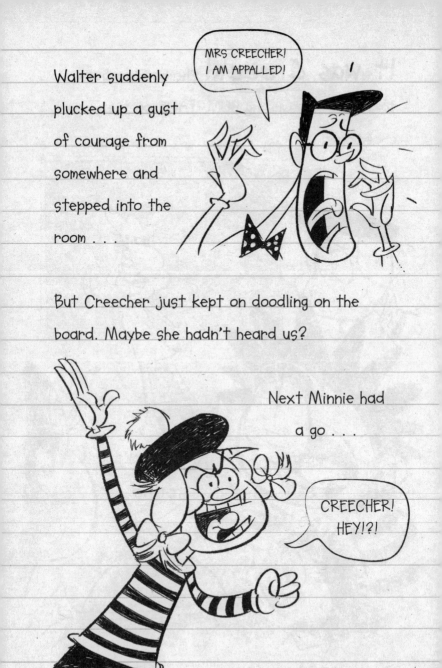

MRS CREECHER! I AM APPALLED!

But Creecher just kept on doodling on the board. Maybe she hadn't heard us?

Next Minnie had a go . . .

CREECHER! HEY!?!

Mrs Creecher still didn't seem to hear us, so I thought I'd try shouting . . . Y'know . . . just to see . . .

OY! BUM-FACE!

Mrs Creecher slowly turned round and shuffled towards her desk. Before we could stop her, she grabbed it by the edge and flipped it over . . . **We all gasped**, but it was then that we noticed her eyes were closed. Creecher tilted her head back and let rip a **big, fat** snoring sound.

SHE WAS ASLEEP!

The crusty old grunion was **sleep-MENACING!**

So that was the mystery over, my merry band of Menaces.

Old Creecher had been so shocked by reading my diaries that she started acting out in her sleep all the **BRILLIANT** menacing lessons she'd learned.

Sergeant Slipper eventually arrived at Bash Street School and woke the Booky Bum-Face up. He took her down to Beanotown Police Station, but they eventually let her go because apparently you can't be blamed for something you do in your sleep . . .

Which gives me the
BEST idea ever!

CAN'T GET INTO TROUBLE FOR
ANYTHING YOU DO IN YOUR SLEEP????

I'VE GOT THE REST OF THE SCHOOL
HOLIDAYS AND LOADS OF MENACING
TO BE GETTING ON WITH . . . ONLY
THIS TIME . . . I'M DOING IT WITH MY
EYES CLOSED!! HA!

WHY NOT DO YOUR OWN MENACE JOURNAL?

I've menaced my diary . . . now it's time to menace yours!

Join *The Beano* comic's front-page legend as he guides you through everything you need to know to create a book just like his. Your teacher will hate it!

STICKY MAYHEM WITH THE BEANO GANG!

Packed to the rafters with puzzles, activities, funnies and over one thousand stickers of all your Beano favourites, from Dennis and Gnasher to Calamity James and the Bash Street Kids.